Painting the Wind

by Michelle Dionetti

Illustrated by Kevin Hawkes

Little, Brown and Company

Boston   New York   Toronto   London

Author's Note

In September of 1888, Vincent van Gogh wrote in a letter to his brother, Theo, "I am very lucky to have a very faithful charwoman. . . . She is quite old and has many and varied offspring, and she keeps my tiles clean and red." I have imagined the charwoman's youngest child to be Claudine, and a help to her mother at the Yellow House at La Place Lamartine. Surely Claudine saw each one of Vincent's paintings, and helped him ready the house for a special visitor, the painter Paul Gauguin.

For Henry Hensche and Sandra Seibel-Bart,
my mentors
M. D.

To Karen,
who has vision
K. H.

Text copyright © 1996 by Michelle Dionetti
Illustrations copyright © 1996 by Kevin Hawkes

First Edition

Library of Congress Cataloging-in-Publication Data.

Dionetti, Michelle
  Painting the wind / by Michelle Dionetti ; illustrated by Kevin Hawkes — 1st ed.
    p. cm.
  Summary: Entranced by the paintings of the unconventional artist Vincent van Gogh, for whom her mother is working as a housekeeper, Claudine is saddened when the townspeople turn against him.
  ISBN 0-316-18602-3
  1. Gogh, Vincent van, 1853–1890—Juvenile fiction. [1. Gogh, Vincent van, 1853–1890—Fiction. 2. Artists—Fiction.]
  I. Hawkes, Kevin, ill. II. Title.
  PZ7.D6214Pai 1996
  [Fic]—dc20   95-5301

10 9 8 7 6 5 4 3 2 1

NIL

Published simultaneously in Canada by Little, Brown & Company (Canada) Limited

Printed in Italy

Calligraphy by Barbara Bash

The paintings for this book were done in oils on acid-free museum board.

In 1888, when horses drew wagons through the stone streets, Claudine lived in the city of Arles, in the south of France. The streets of Arles were built narrow and crooked to keep out the blazing sun. But nothing could keep out the wind. The mistral, they called it, and it blew then as it does now, as though it were made of rage.

Claudine was the last child of many, and all in her family worked, for times were poor. Her father worked on the barges on the River Rhône. Her brothers and sisters worked in the orchards and farms in the country surrounding Arles. Claudine wished to be outside, too, where she could lift her face up to the wind and the sun. But for now she worked indoors with her mother, cleaning other people's houses.

One morning Maman led Claudine past the ancient Roman arena, where crowds roared at the bullfights every Sunday. Claudine longed to climb its three arched tiers. From the top she could see over the jumble of red tile roofs to the green and blue countryside, and the yellow sky that hung over all. But Maman had a new house to clean, and she hurried Claudine through the narrow streets to the River Rhône, where it crooked like an elbow at La Place Lamartine.

In the Yellow House on La Place Lamartine lived a painter. His neighbors called him Vincent. The children called him Fou Roux, Redheaded Fool, because of his red-gold hair and because he painted outside, even on days when the sun was blistering hot, even on days when the mistral made the trees bend sideways and blew chimneys from the roofs.

"Stay out of the painter's way," whispered Maman. "He is crazy. The mistral has blown away his mind."

And so Claudine kept quiet as a mouse while she scrubbed the red tile floors. The Yellow House smelled of oil paints. Canvases leaned on all the walls, and while Claudine worked, she looked her fill. Vincent's paintings did not look like other paintings, neat and perfect. They were thick and wild. Bright suns curled in spangled light. Sunflowers blared like little trumpets.

"So beautiful, Maman!" she whispered.

But Maman muttered under her breath about crazy men who called themselves artists. When Vincent came in with a painting under his arm, his shirtsleeve smeared with yellow, Maman sent Claudine outside to wash the front step.

As they walked home from the Yellow House, Maman told Claudine she must always work hard and not be foolish like the painter.

"Yes, Maman," said Claudine dreamily.

She was only half listening. Something was happening to her eyes. The trees no longer looked green to her, but gold and purple and orange and blue, and their branches danced like flames.

The people of Arles worked hard, but at night they stopped, and on Sundays they rested. Claudine wondered if Vincent ever rested. She found him painting in the ancient Roman graveyard. She spied him painting by the quay. She discovered him at the river where she and Maman did the family washing, painting the women at work. His women were hunched like turtles. His river was a flowing blue curve. The sky he made was green, and over it a yellow sun spun in circles.

Claudine stood behind Vincent, watching until she hungered to make a painting, too. She ran to Maman's side and took up one of Papa's shirts. She swirled it round and round in the cold water, turning it like Vincent's sun.

At home Claudine thought of the drawings she'd seen in the Yellow House. She wanted to make drawings like that, where the sky was not an empty space, but full of clouds and birds wheeling.

She took charred wood from the fireplace and bent to draw on the stone floor. She tried to draw trees with strong black marks like Vincent's. She tried to make the branches bend and the leaves take flight. But she felt clumsy. The charcoal smudged. She could not make a tree come alive at all.

All through the harvest, Claudine worked around new wet canvases at the Yellow House. While men and women gathered fruit and grain, Vincent's crop of paintings grew and grew. When the sun burned down red, setting fire to the red tile roofs, Vincent painted the sky red with color straight from his tubes. When the sun burned down yellow, he painted the sun, the sky, the fields yellow. When the mistral blew, Vincent tied his easel to the ground with rope to keep his canvas from blowing over. When rain drove him inside, still he painted: sunflowers, boots, his food before he ate it. Like the wind, he was driven.

"I saw Fou Roux at the orchard today," said one of Claudine's brothers at dinner. "He was painting the olive trees purple!"

Claudine let the others laugh. Perhaps she would see the purple trees leaning against a wall in the Yellow House.

"They say he paints at night!" said one of her sisters.

"Yes, I have seen him," said Papa, "with a straw hat on his head and burning candles in the brim. He claims to paint by the candlelight! The wind has blown away his mind."

"The wind," said Maman, "or the liquor he drinks."

Claudine remembered Vincent's painting of the night café, the blues and oranges, the strange people silent and dark. She wished she could make paintings that could talk without words, as Vincent did. She wished she could make a painting of Vincent that would show her family what she saw inside him.

In October Vincent covered the inside walls of the Yellow House with a new coat of whitewash.

"We have to make the house ready!" he cried. "My friend Paul is coming to stay."

When Claudine went upstairs to sweep, she saw that the spare room was newly whitewashed and paintings of sunflowers were hung on the walls. In Vincent's room, the bed and chairs were painted the color of butter, and the windowsills were painted green. A bright red cloth covered the bed, and a blue basin stood on the orange table.

"A crazy room!" muttered Maman. "It gives me a headache!"

But Claudine thought she would love a room like Vincent's, bright as summer.

Soon there was another painter at the Yellow House. His name was Paul. Eagerly Claudine followed the painters to an orchard one noon. They set up their easels near the apple trees and began to paint. Soon she saw that Paul also used vivid colors, though his were deep rather than bright. Vincent's colors were shouts, and Paul's were singing voices.

"Not like that!" cried Vincent when he looked at Paul's work. "You miss the violet shadow here! Am I not right, my young friend?" he called to Claudine.

Claudine saw Vincent's violet in the tree's shadow. Paul had painted his shadow blue, and she thought she saw that, too. Then she saw her own color.

"It's purple!" she said. "With red mixed in!"

But neither man heard her. They were arguing angrily about which of them was right.

On Christmas Day bells rang all over Arles. While her family prepared for church, Claudine ran outside to feed bread to the pigeons whose song filled the courtyard. *"Coo-roo,"* sang the pigeons. *"Coo-roo, coo-roo."* Claudine scattered crumbs and watched the sun paint the buildings gold.

After Mass Claudine and her family strolled through Arles to greet their friends. Horses drew wagons through the streets. Happy shouts filled the air.

A crowd of people thronged the square in front of the Yellow House. Their shrill voices frightened Claudine. Had something happened to Vincent? She pushed through them.

"Is something wrong?" she cried.

"They have taken Fou Roux away," the people replied. "Fou Roux and his friend had a fight, and Vincent cut off the lobe of his own ear."

For many weeks Claudine could not go to the Yellow House. No one was there. Dust gathered inside. His neighbors were glad that Vincent was gone, but Claudine was not glad. She worked with Maman day after day and wished the sun could give off more light.

At the close of winter, the painter returned to the Yellow House. Claudine and Maman returned, too, to clean. Claudine thought sadly that Vincent seemed tired. The joy had gone from his eyes. He could not bring himself to paint but often slumped at the window, gazing across La Place Lamartine.

One day while she scrubbed, Claudine heard shouting.
"Fou Roux, Fou Roux!" the children chanted.
Claudine looked up in dismay. Would they never leave Vincent alone?
Vincent opened the window and yelled, but the children kept chanting, "Fou Roux, Fou Roux." Hurt and enraged, Vincent threw his chair out the window, then some paintings.
"Oh, no!" cried Claudine.
She grabbed the painter's arm.

The youths scattered. Adults ran from the nearby café, shaking their fists and shouting at Vincent. Maman pushed Claudine out of the Yellow House. Under the feet of angry men, Claudine found a small painting of Vincent's two battered shoes. She set it carefully out of harm's way.

"Come away from there!" said Maman.

"Those men are not fair to Vincent," Claudine said boldly. She felt her face grow hot.

"You are as foolish as that painter!" scolded Maman.

But Claudine could not keep still. "The boys were mean!" she said. "They called him names!"

"What of it?" said Maman. "A man does not care if children call him names."

But Claudine thought that anyone would care.

Vincent's neighbors had become afraid of him. They signed a petition to ban him from living in the Yellow House. The magistrate granted their request.

When the time came for Vincent to leave, the neighbors gathered to watch and gossip. Claudine did not want to stand with them. She pushed through the whispering crowd and knocked on the door of the Yellow House.

The crowd quieted. The door opened a crack.

"Well?" said Vincent. His eyes were sad.

"I came to tell you I like your paintings," said Claudine loudly.

A tiny light came into Vincent's eyes. "Do not tell the others," he joked, "or they will make you leave, too!"

He handed Claudine a small painting. Sunflowers blazed from it in curls of light.

"For you," he said.

Claudine hugged the painting and ran home. She understood that Vincent had said good-bye, and she clenched her teeth to keep from crying. But in her heart she felt glad. She felt as strong as the sun, as fierce as the mistral. Vincent had given her the eyes to see the heart of a sunflower, brave and bold and filled with fire.